A
POWER
FAMILIES
ADVENTURE

For Lilu - S.M.
For Drew - A.E.

Russell DeLeon, Executive Producer
With Special Thanks To Our Renewable Energy Champions:
Turner Foundation, Inc.
Stephen Cordova

Jack Hook Publishing
1288 Columbus Ave, #279
San Francisco, CA 94133

First U.S. Edition: 2011
Library of Congress Control Number: 2011933266
ISBN: 978-0-9837863-1-3

10 9 8 7 6 5 4 3 2 1
Printed in the United States of America

MAX POWER and the Bagpipes

A POWER FAMILIES Adventure

Story by
SUSE MOORE

Illustrated by
ANDY ELKERTON

Jack hook

High on a hill where the north wind blows
Max was making snowballs.

"Watch me, Haggis. I am Max the juggler!" he said,
throwing two snowballs into the air.

SPLOT! SPLAT!

both snowballs landed on his head
just as Grandpa Power's boat
pulled into the harbor below.

Max and Haggis jumped onto
their snowboard and raced
down through the wind fields.

SWISH! SWOOSH!
through the snow they swooped, carving a fresh track.

"Hang on, Haggis!" shouted Max.
"We're going to catch some air!"

WOOSH!

the snowboard took off...

BUMP! they landed in a pile of snow on the jetty.
"Ahoy, Max!" waved Grandpa from the deck.
"Are you sure you're ready to do your circus show?"

"I will be," said Max.

Nippy Knot

Grandpa looked up at the wind turbines and raised a bushy eyebrow. "We will need more wind to make enough electricity to heat that circus tent."

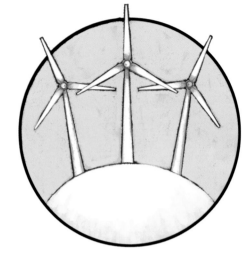

"But the circus has its own power generator," said Max.

WIND METER

"Great! Then let's get ready for your juggling show," said Grandpa.

Back at the house Max threw
two golf balls up into the air.

"I am Max the juggler!" he said.

He caught one but the other bounced
off the ceiling with a PING!

PLOP!
the ball landed in Grandpa's porridge.

"Arrgghh!" said Grandpa.
"You definitely need more practice."

Just then Max's Dad walked in.
"You can stop juggling," he said.
"The circus power generator
has broken down and
they've cancelled the show."

"But why?" said Max.
"All the village power is needed
to keep our buildings warm," said Dad.

"Your school,

your friends' homes,

the Post Office,

and Scotty's Shop."

Max's heart sank like a stone.

"I'm sorry," said Dad. "If we could get the wind to blow harder then we could generate enough electricity for the circus tent too."

"It's not fair!" said Max, running up the stairs to his room.

Max sat on his bed. It was the worst day ever.
"Ahoy, Max!" said Grandpa, knocking on the door.

Out on the icy ocean aboard the Nippy Knot, Max helped Grandpa search through his old sea chest.

"Here it is," said Grandpa, opening a tin box and handing Max a piece of paper.

" 'Powers' Blowing Tune' to be played at sunset at the top of Spike Hill," read Max.

"You'll need these too," said Grandpa, unhooking a pair of dusty bagpipes from the wall.

"WOOSH!" replied the wind, whistling over the sea and up the hill toward the music.

"La-la-me-la-la-me!" sang the bagpipes. The wind howled and snatched at the Blowing Tune. "No!" cried Max.

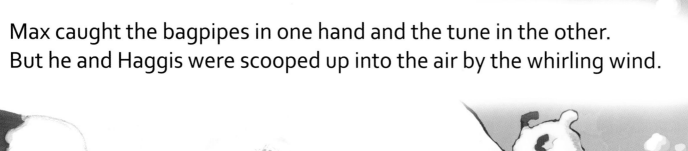

Max caught the bagpipes in one hand and the tune in the other.
But he and Haggis were scooped up into the air by the whirling wind.

Round and round they spun.

The blades of the wind turbines accelerated, generating more and more electricity.

All of a sudden the whirlwind spun off the top of the hill.

"Help!" cried Max. "We're being blown out to sea!"

But when the whirlwind
reached Grandpa's boat
it unfurled, landing Max and Haggis

gently on the deck.

"Phew!" said Max.
"Nice work. You both did a great job getting the wind to blow. There's going to be plenty of electricity now to heat the big tent," said Grandpa.

And the very next evening...

In the brightly-lit, toasty-warm, big tent Max juggled three golf balls at once.
The audience cheered.

"That's my grandson!" shouted Grandpa.
"The windmaker and the juggler!"
"Woof! Woof!" barked Haggis.

THE END.